DISCLAIMER

This is a work of fiction. Names, characters, businesses, places, events, and incidents are either the products of the author's imagination or used in a fictitious manner. Any resemblance to actual persons, living or dead, or actual events is purely coincidental.

CW01499768

For Literally Lovesick

ACKNOWLEDGEMENTS

These books exist within a multiverse consisting of multiple books with crossing stories narrative and timelines. We want to thank everyone who has helped bring the Literally Lovesick Universe to life, the contributors and the readers.

Please continue to support us and join us on social media. Literally Lovesick can be found on Twitter, Tumblr, Facebook, Instagram & of course Youtube where you can find some great free quality content.

Thank you

PROLOGUE

Sept. 7, 2019

I cannot believe this just happened. It was supposed to be a dull day today, but instead, I got blindsided. Today was my older sister, Hattie's engagement party. It was supposed to be all about how she is marrying the love of her life since she was sixteen. A typical cliché about how the guy she loved in high school didn't even know she existed until ten years later. Now after dating for four years, they were finally getting married. It all should have been a happy, easy day. Assuming you ignore the fact that I can't stand her fiancé. Never have and never will. Christopher was a pompous ass who only loved himself. How my sister ever thought he was the perfect guy for her, I'll never understand. But who knows what will happen now thanks to my bitch of a best friend who just announced to everyone how Christopher and I slept together one night three years ago! One drunken night three years ago. Quite possibly the biggest mistake I have ever made, and now it was being thrown back in my face by my own best friend. I thought she was my best friend, turns out I'm a really crappy judge of character, more so than I thought anyways. See, this is why I prefer to be alone. People are shady and untrusting. They will lie right to your face and tell you how they would never tell a soul.

Only for them to wait until you are in a room surrounded by your family and your family's closest friends to spill everything. Like telling a room full of people at my sister's engagement party how I had sex with the soon to be groom.

So much for best friends. I can't believe Ali would do this to me. After ten years of friendship, she threw it all away and for what? I seriously have no idea why she would do this to me. None. She knew I don't trust people very easily. She knew I wasn't one to have a hoard of friends. I preferred to be alone and keep to myself, so why would she do this? Now I have no friends and my family are beyond pissed at me. They were all acting like I was some common whore on the corner. It was one drunken night, but apparently that doesn't matter. It doesn't matter that I've never really done anything with a man. Christopher was my second guy that I had slept with in my twenty-five years of life. And I don't even remember it. The one boyfriend I had in high school was a joke. We had sex all of four times and I gave him head once. We lasted all of six months before he was off to bang the cheerleading squad. I'm the furthest thing from a whore. But does that matter to my family? Nope. All they care about is their precious firstborn being traumatized by this whole experience. Like I'm not?

People suck. I've been thinking about a change, maybe now is the perfect time for it.

A fresh start somewhere else, in a place where no one knows me. I can just be Issy. And not the slut that slept with my sister's fiancé. I think a fresh start is exactly what I need.

CHAPTER 1

Dec. 31, 2019

It's been almost four months now since I left Birmingham and moved to London. At first, I wasn't too sure it was the right place, but now I really like it. I'm liking that it's enormous compared to Birmingham. Over eight million people live here so it's a massive city with so many beautiful things to see. I'm really liking it and all of the culture. I got a new job working as a server in a high-end fancy restaurant. The pay is good, and the tips are great. I got a lovely one-bedroom apartment not too far from the Blackheath area. It was the perfect size and let all of my current furniture fit in it without having to give any away. The first few months I went around getting myself familiar with the city and finding all the great places to get a coffee or some pizza. My co-workers are nice, but I keep them as just co-workers. I'm not looking to make a big group of friends. If I had it my way, I wouldn't have any friends, but Scarlett wouldn't let that happen.

The owner of the restaurant that I work at, he also owns a gay club that I've worked at a handful of times when he is short on staff. At first, I wasn't too sure. I had never been to a gay club before.

I'm not against gay people, but I had never known any. It was an eye-opening experience to say the least. But a good one.

I am glad that I went that first time, and the tips were great. Now I don't hesitate when my boss asks me to cover a shift over there. I met Scarlett there that first night; she was very different from my last best friend. Or any of my previous friends for that matter. She's a wild child. She loves to party and do recreational drugs. She is also not one to shy away from sex. I can't even count how many times I've walked in on her and some girl in the ladies' room at the club. She might seem crazy to most people, the old me would have agreed, but there is something freeing when your whole family refuses to talk to you and you have no friends. There's no judgements. There's no one there to tell you what to do and how to behave. For the first time in my life, I have the freedom just to be me. The problem is, I don't really know who that is.

It's why tonight I agreed to go out with Scarlett and have some fun. Tonight, I'm wearing a sexy red dress that has a deep V-neck and only goes to my mid-thigh, and I'm wearing red high heels with it. My mother would literally kill me if she saw me in it, and I only bought it after Scarlett convinced me I needed to show off my body more. It was an impulse buy, but tonight I'm glad I did.

Tonight, I'm going to a club and I'm not going to stress about how I look or how I dance.

I'm not going to think about if the guy who is asking me to dance is someone I can take to meet my parents. Tonight is about fun. It's about being a single, good looking twenty-five-year-old woman just out with her friend to celebrate the New Year. And if I get drunk, then so what? I'm not working tomorrow anyway. And who knows, maybe I'll actually have something exciting to write about tomorrow.

9

Noticing the time, I only had thirty minutes to finish up getting ready before Scarlett would be here. I still had to do my hair and makeup, and that was not something I wanted to do with her here. I would end up looking like some doped up clown that had just been released from the circus. Scarlett had a different style than me in that sense. She loved her bold colours and was often changing her hair to have different coloured highlights in it. It looked great on her, but it wouldn't on me. Putting my diary away, I headed off to my bathroom to finish getting ready.

Thirty minutes later there was a thud at my door, and I knew exactly who it was. Scarlett always had a knock that sounded like someone was chasing her down. It was never just one simple knock, not with this girl.

It was a set of ten fast knocks like you couldn't hear the first nine. And if you didn't answer after a few seconds you were getting it all over again, only that time she wouldn't stop until the door was opened.
It had pissed off Ms Whittley a few times, and at eighty she was not in the mood for much in life. Opening my door, there was Scarlett in all her glory. If I thought my dress was short and revealing, hers left nothing to the imagination. A silver dress covered in glitter that went down to the top of her thigh, just enough to cover any of her important parts down below. The dress was backless, and the front was a silver sheer that only had two small circles of a glitter cluster where her nipples were. I had to admit though, she always looked sexy in anything that she wore. It was really no surprise why all the girls loved her.

"Hey, you ready hot stuff?" Scarlett asked with a flirty smile.

"As I'll ever be. You sure about this club? I heard it could get pretty wild." I asked, closing and locking my door.

"It'll be fine. And wild is the best part. We're getting you a man tonight honey." Scarlett put her arm through mine, and we were off to the cab.

"I'm not looking for a date."

"Fine, we're getting you some dick tonight," Scarlett said with a giggle.

"What am I going to do with you?" I asked, with my own smile. "I can think of a few things, but I don't think you're ready to hear them. Look, tonight is about fun. And fun has no rules. So just enjoy yourself and let loose. Who knows, you might actually have some fun tonight."

"I promised I wouldn't think tonight and just let myself have some fun. You just make sure to text me if you head off with someone. I don't want to spend the night trying to find you and make sure some serial killer didn't get you." I lectured. It was not the first time that we had gone out and Scarlett left to me wait around and wonder where she was.

"I promise." Scarlett waved a cab down, and we were off. I had no idea what was going to happen tonight, but one thing I did know. I was excited to see what the night had in store for me.

CHAPTER 2

The first thing I noticed was the loud music blaring out from the building. We weren't even inside yet, and I could hear the song perfectly. I had no idea what it was, some type of club dance music, but the people in line seemed to really enjoy it. I was about to head over to the end of the line, but Scarlett pulled my arm.

"Honey, we're hot, we don't wait in line."

I could have argued that there were other attractive looking females, but with Scarlett, there was no point. Heading over to the bouncer, a very attractive muscular man I must say, Scarlett made sure her hips were swaying and she had on a killer smile.

"Hey Hot stuff, care to let us in?" Scarlett said with a sultry voice.

"For two beauties like you, I think I can make that happen. But only if Red promises me a dance." He said with a wink in my direction.

It took me a moment to release he was calling me red because of my dress; I have brown hair after all. Acting braver than I felt, I said: "I can do that."

"You better hurry though, she's way too hot to be alone for long," Scarlett added.

"I'll be in there soon." The bouncer opened the door and we headed inside.

The club looked like every other club out there. There wasn't anything too special about it. But it was packed. I had a feeling that the people in line were never going to be getting in. Not on New Year's Eve. We made quick work of ordering our drinks, I wasn't much of a drinker, but I was a fan of a martini. And I was planning on having a lot of them tonight, a little bit of liquid courage never hurt anyone. I turned around and saw that Scarlett was already out on the dance floor stuck between two women. I couldn't help the chuckle that came up. Never wasted time. Quickly finishing my drink, I decided to join her. Tonight, was about fun and I wasn't going to be having any of it by standing around here.

I don't know how many drinks later or how long it was before I felt strong arms wrap themselves around me. I turned to see that it was the bouncer and he gave me one hell of a smile. I should have said something, my mind was telling me I was supposed to do something, but all I could do was sway to the music. I also couldn't help but notice that he had a growing bulge in the front of his pants. Letting myself go, I pushed back against it and grinded my ass into it even more. I was rewarded with a groan.

"I don't have long on my break; what do you say we take this dance into the backroom?"
His voice was right by my ear, and it sent a shiver down my spine. I should have said no, but my body was screaming for more, so I gave the nod, and we were off. He easily guided me through the swarm of people into the back breakroom. It was empty of people, but there was a couch and a table. You could

still hear the music coming from the club. He sat down on the couch and pulled me down on top of him, so I was straddling his lap. I started to move to the music, rolling my hips and grinding against his denim-covered hard on. He gave another deep groan and ran his hands to my ass, pushing my dress up to reveal my red thong underneath. He gave my ass a playful smack that had a moan escaping my mouth before he moved and pushed the top of my dress away from my braless chest. His mouth instantly found my nipples and started to suck on them. I moved my own hands down to his pants and quickly freed his hard dick.

Placing his hands on my ass, he pushed me forward so my hips would grind directly into him. The friction was unlike anything I had ever felt before, and considering I had already had sex, that was saying something. I moved my hips even faster against him, forgetting all about the music or the possibility that someone could walk in on us at any moment.

He began to grind his hips up to meet mine, and I knew he was just as enthralled as I was.
I made sure to put enough pressure on my clit to help throw me over the edge. We were both getting close ; our movements became more frantic, more needy. I was the first one to go over the edge, giving a long moan as I felt the pulsing inside of me. A moment later, he was squeezing my ass, and I could feel him pulsing right along with me. My own cum soaking the inside of my panties and his soaking the outside. It should have bothered me, but I found it turning me on even more.

A second to catch our breaths and then Mr Bouncer, did his pants back up as he spoke.

"I gotta get back out there. Thanks for the dance Sweetheart."

Still a little hazed I just gave a nod and got up. I quickly fixed myself, and then we headed out of the room. He promptly went back towards the door to get on with the rest of his shift.

CHAPTER 3

Jan. 1, 2020

Is it possible for your head to explode? I mean actually explode. I swear it's going to happen any second from now and all Scarlett will find is my headless body holding some stupid pen lying in bed. After drinking for four years, I finally have my first hangover. Why I thought drinking eight martinis in four hours was a good idea, I'll never know. I swear there should have been someone there to tell me it was stupid. Where was my fairy godmother last night on martini number six? Eight martinis might not seem like much to most people, but when you only drink one or two every six months, it's a big deal.

This hangover is not even the worst of my problems. I have no idea how I feel about what I did last night. I wish I could blame it on the alcohol, but I went out looking for some fun and that is exactly what I found, but I didn't expect it to go that way and I didn't expect it to leave me feeling like this. Confused. Torn. I just barely remember getting home last night, alone as Scarlett was already off with some other girl. I took my dress and shoes off, and fell into bed, leaving my cum soaked thong on. Even now, it's still on and I know I should be grossed out and scrubbing myself clean in the shower. But I don't want to. Wearing it, even now, kinda makes me feel empowered in a way. And a little turned on. That's the confusing part.

Everything that I was raised to believe about how a woman should act by my mother goes against everything I feel right now. I don't feel like some dirty slut. I don't feel like I'm going to spend the rest of my eternal life in Hell being poked by hot pokers. I feel empowered. Ok, there is a little bit of shame and embarrassment underneath all of that, but maybe that's normal. I felt that way after the first time I had Scotty's condom covered dick in my mouth. Perhaps that's from my mother's voice in my head constantly telling me how to act and what a proper lady is like.

If I think about this logically, what I did last night was really quite tame compared to what others would be doing. I didn't have sex with him; I barely touched him. Hell, we didn't even kiss. It really wasn't that bad, and it did feel good.

Really good. Like I'm still turned on by it good. Maybe Scarlett is right ; perhaps I should be exploring my sexuality and seeing what is out there. Who could it really hurt? Ok well myself, but if I'm the only one being hurt by it, then that's my own fault. It's not like anything I decide to do wouldn't be my decision. I'm a young woman, who is exploring her sexuality, that seems perfectly normal to me. It's not like I'm going to start going to those sex clubs that Scarlett loves to go to. I'm just not going to shut myself out anymore. I'm not going to deny myself the opportunities that come up. I get asked out all the time at work, I'm not interested in dating, but maybe they aren't either.

My whole life, I have been sheltered and told what to do and what not to do. Living a stuffy life where you had to have your body covered and no tight clothing. I always did what I was told and expected to do. But screw it. They don't want to talk to me. They want to pretend like I don't exist all because of one drunken mistake. A mistake they are blaming me for and not even him. Hattie still has pictures of them on her Facebook page. They are still getting married. I'm not invited anymore and, if Hattie knew I could still see her Facebook page, I'm sure I would be blocked from it. If she wants to marry a man that cheated on her, that's her problem. I'm done living by their rules and expectations. It's time I got to discover who I am and what my own expectations were. It's time to live for me.

Assuming my head doesn't explode.

CHAPTER 4

Jan. 3, 2020

Scarlett is relentless. I told her I had to work this evening and yet she won't stop calling and texting me every five minutes trying to get me to call in sick so we can go and party. I just saw her two days ago, and she already wants to hang out. I should be used to it by now. After I met her two months ago, she's been coming around more and more. At first, it was hard to get used to, but now it's just normal. She has a bad day, she's here. She has a good day, she's here. She's bored, she's here. I think I made my point. It's not often I go out with her, and since going out on New Year's Eve, she's been trying to get me to go out again with her. I might have said yes, but tonight I have to work. It's Friday and a dinner shift at work, which means the tips are going to be good. When I first started working at Legna, all I would get were the morning shifts when they first opened. I had to earn the right to work dinner rush and weekends. Now that I finally have, I wasn't about the throw that all away just to go out and drink with Scarlett. Even if she is my only friend.

Though if I was being honest, there was one person I was looking forward to seeing tonight.

I have no idea what his name is, he's a regular though on Friday night at the restaurant.

I usually get to serve him, and he always pays in cash, so no credit card for me to sneak a peek at for a name. He tips really well, and he always flirts with me. He's what you would call man pretty. Short brown hair, green eyes that look like he could see right into your soul, built, but not overly built like Mr Bouncer. Just enough to know that he worked out and could handle himself in a fight. I had no idea what he did for a living or really anything about him. Anytime I asked him anything remotely personal he always changed the subject. Flipped it around back to my life or the restaurant. After a couple of times, I gave up asking. I had asked a few of the girls that worked there longer than me, but they didn't know any more than I did. He was a mystery, and that only made him sexier.

He had propositioned me before, but I always turned him down. Tonight, I was looking to change that. I did my very first lap dance two days ago, and tonight I was looking for another first. What that would be, I have no idea, but I was excited to find out. I had already picked out my outfit. We were allowed to wear what we wished at the restaurant as long as it was black. My boss didn't care if it was sexy as long as it was tasteful. He encouraged it because it brought in the men that paid well. I usually wore black slacks and a black button-down shirt. Tonight though, I was wearing a tight black shirt that went down to just the top of my mid-thigh, slightly shorter than my red dress. And a black sequin halter top with no back or a bra and pair it all off with my black stiletto heels.

It was going to be a drastic difference, but one that had my nipples hardening at just the thought. Tonight was going to be a good night. I could feel it. And hopefully, by the end of it, I would be feeling a lot more.

It was nearing ten o'clock that night, and I could feel myself getting disappointed. Mr Mystery hadn't shown up yet. He normally showed around eight for a late dinner and a few drinks, but tonight he was a no show. I knew I shouldn't be disappointed; there was no guarantee we would even do anything anyway, but still. We were closed at eleven, and the likelihood of him showing up now was not good. Maybe it wasn't too late to go out and meet up with Scarlett. I was quickly losing hope as I wiped down the last table in my section when Mr Mystery walked through the doors. At just a quarter to eleven, it was too late for him to be getting any food. The kitchen had been closed for the past fifteen minutes so the cooks could clean and head home on time. I was also the last server here. The joys of being the one to close at night.

Mr Mystery headed over to the bar and sat down. I quickly finished wiping down the table and headed over.

"Evening, it's late for you to be here," I said from behind the bar.

"Just needed a drink before I head home."

I loved how rich his voice always sounded. I almost had a slight purr to it. And it never failed to make my body tingle.

"What can I get you?"

Mr Mystery paused for a second and gave me his full attention. As if noticing for the first time what I was wearing compared to what I normally did. His eyes travelled all over my body, want very clear in his eyes.

"Do you want your usual or perhaps you'd prefer something with a sweeter taste?" I said with a flirty smirk. This man wanted me, and I wanted him. Tonight, it was going to be that simple.

"I haven't had dessert yet. I could go for something sweet." He easily flirted back.

I turned around and made a show of my ass swaying as I went over to the whiskey glasses. He bent over to grab the whiskey on the bottom shelf, making sure I didn't bend my knees, not caring that he would be able to see the bottom of my ass cheeks. I could have sworn I heard a groan coming from him. After pouring him a shot, I placed it down in front of him. But I leaned forward, so I was closer to him, giving him a good view of my breasts in the process.

"Fifteen minutes, around back. I'll have your dessert nice and ready for you."

"I like my dessert wet and without any containers, but I will take the container home."

I knew he was referring to my thong, normally I would be outraged at the idea of going pantyless or having a man keep a pair, but tonight it only turned me on.

"I'll see you then," I said, before turning away and getting the rest of my work finished.

Fifteen minutes later, I was the last one left to leave. After quickly locking up, I went into the ladies' room and removed my black thong. It was drenched in my juices from just the thought of what was going to happen around back. I quickly thought about how once again I would be doing something where someone could see us, but again I didn't care. I quickly left the ladies room and grabbed my purse and headed out back. Sure enough Mr Mystery was already out there waiting for me.

"Do you have my dessert?" He asked, coming closer to me.

"I do."

"Put your leg up on either side." He said, nodding to the crates we had outside.
There was one to my right and to my left, it would put me taller, though I figured that was what he wanted. I did as he said and only then did, he speak again.

"Show me my dessert."

I lifted the bottom of my shirt all the way up so he could see me. He groaned when he saw that I was fully waxed. A new thing I had decided to do just yesterday. Scarlett had said a lot of guys liked it. Judging by the hunger in his eyes, I had to agree. He came over to me and bent down so he was at eye level with my quim. He ran his finger down the front of it and in between my folds.

"Oh, so wet. Just how I like it. But how sweet do you taste?"

That was the only warning I got before his tongue was pushing between my folds. I couldn't stop the moan. His hands went to my hips and pushed me down, spreading me open even more and with my legs further apart, I was completely at his mercy. His tongue pushed inside my hole and I couldn't stop the moans that flooded out of me. He was completely devouring me with his tongue as he thrust it in and out of me. I could vaguely hear a zipper before he was pulling his erection out and jerking off as he ate away at my quim. His tongue made its way to my clit, and he sucked at it, pulling the swollen bud into his mouth.

My hands made their way into his hair, and I couldn't stop my hips from rocking forward. He gave a small growl and his pace increased.

"Oh fuck." I moaned.

I needed more ; I wanted more. His tongue was back inside my hole, even deeper than before. He was thrusting in and out of me as he jerked himself off. I could feel the pressure building in my stomach. And when he moved his free hand over to my clit and started to rub it in time with his thrusts, I saw black spots crawling across my sight as I came hard and long. He gave a deep moan as my cum hit his tongue. His tongue continued to lick at everything I was giving him. After I stopped pulsing, he stood up and pulled me into a heated kiss. I moaned as his tongue invaded my mouth, tasting myself on him. He was quickly jerking himself off and after a moment he came with a long groan. I could feel his hot cum hitting just above my quim. He pulled back from my mouth and was breathing heavy; we both were.

After a moment, he pulled back and put himself back together. I did the same and stepped down off the crates. I quickly fixed my skirt, and then he spoke.

"My container?" He had a flirty smirk on his face once again. It should have annoyed me, but it didn't.

I pulled out my black thong, and he took it with a smile.

"Very sexy." He came right up against my mouth before he spoke. "You ever want to do this again, hand me your panties when I'm in, and I'll know." And then he was kissing me with everything in him. I didn't think I would ever get tired of his searing kiss.

All too soon, he pulled back. "You got a safe way home?"

"I'm good."

"Yes, you are." He said with a smirk as he pulled back and started to head back to his car.

Leaving me alone to try and get my legs to work.

CHAPTER 5

Jan. 4, 2020

It's 10 AM on a Saturday and I'm still in bed. Something that doesn't tend to happen very often. Normally I'm up and cleaning like a good girl. My mother always said it was important to keep your home clean and in perfect condition. After all, you had no idea who could come by at a moment's notice, and you should never have a messy home. Certain things were drilled into my head from growing up, things that didn't really matter in the long run, but stayed anyway. It was one of those things I had been working on fixing since moving here.

Now what I want to think about was last night. My mind is still blown by the amazing feeling of having Mr Mystery's tongue inside of me. My one and only boyfriend Scott, has seriously robbed me. He never went down on me, and now I feel like I should be suing him for emotional distress or something. And Mr Mystery was all for another round, hell yes! If he's that good with his tongue, I can't imagine how good he is with his dick. I swear it is like everything is brighter this morning. Like my eyes couldn't work properly until I've had a tongue thoroughly ravishing my quim. I wanted more. And unlike last time, I have no shame in me.

I should, we did fool around in a spot where once again we could have been caught, but knowing that made it all the more exciting. I want more. I want to feel everything that I've been missing out on. I want to embrace being a woman and my sexuality.

My phone rang, snapping me out of my thoughts. I put my pen down and picked up my phone, Scarlett.

"Hey Scarlett, how are you?"

"Good. You missed one hell of a time last night."

"I'm surprised you're even awake this early." I teased.

"I haven't gone to bed yet." Scarlett giggled, and I knew she was still high. Not surprising.

"You should sleep then."

"In a minute. How was work last night?"

"It was fine. Mr Mystery came by very late last night, just before closing."

"God, that man is hot. I'm gay and even I know he's hot. Still no name yet?"

"Nope. But he did have dessert around the back after closing."

I couldn't help the smile that spread across my face at just the mention of what had happened. I had told Scarlett that I had been thinking about opening myself up more in sexual terms. She was all for it, and it felt really nice to have a friend be so open about it and supportive.

"Dessert as in cheesecake or as in you?"

"Definitely not cheesecake."

I had to pull the phone away from my ear as Scarlett squealed.

"Oh my god, tell me everything!"

"Not much happened. We didn't have sex, but he did go down on me, which was better than any sex I have ever had. I mean, it was earth-shattering. The world actually shattered all around us."

"I still can't believe you've never had a guy eat you out before. I mean really that's so rude of them. So that's all you did?"

"He kissed me and jerked himself off, which was a little disappointing because I would have loved to do that for him. He seemed caught up in everything. He did say that he would love a repeat."

"And would you love one?"
"Yes, I would. Though, not in a back alley would be nice. Am I crazy for wanting to do it again? I mean he is a complete stranger; I don't even know his name."

"So what? You had fun, right?"

"Yeah."

"You enjoyed it, right?"

"Oh yeah."

"Then who cares if you know his name or if he knows your name. The whole point is to have fun. As long as you both are consensual adults, who cares? Screw half of the city's male population if you want. As long as you are enjoying yourself, that's all that matters hot stuff. Get out of your head and have some fun sexy time."

"You're right. Thanks. We still on for dinner tomorrow?"

"Yes, all good. Have fun at work tonight and let me know if Mr Mystery shows up."

"I will, but he normally only comes on Friday night. But a girl can dream."

"Hell yeah, they can. And you better be making those dreams a reality."
"I'll try my best. Everything good with you?"

"Oh, you know me."

I did know her. She usually had something going on. Something that would blow up in her face and I would hear all about it. It used to annoy the hell out of me, but I got used to it. Just like I got used to her always randomly showing up and raiding my kitchen for food.

"That I do. Be safe tonight if you go out."

"Always."

"Get some sleep."

"I will, eventually." Scarlett giggled once again, and I knew she was going to be up for a few more hours at least.

"Bye."

"Bye-bye."

I hung up the phone with a slight eye roll. That girl was going to dig herself an early grave, I swear. I was all for experiencing new things in my life right now, but I was not going to be doing what Scarlett was. My phone beeped again, but this time it was a text message. It was from an unknown number.

I know what you are doing. I'm always watching you.

Creepy, but whoever this was clearly had the wrong number. I deleted the text and decided it was a good time to get on with my day. I had work in four hours, so I really needed to get something to eat and take a shower. It also would be good to get some groceries as well. Without a second thought about that text message, I got my day started.

CHAPTER 6

Jan. 19, 2020

Oh my god, I don't even know where to start with what happened last night. With my first Saturday off in a while I agreed to go out to the gay club for fun with Scarlett. She's been dating this new girl. Not too sure I like her, but Scarlett seems to be all into her right now. And with me being on my period I knew I wouldn't have to worry about any guy trying to pick me up. Side note, I haven't seen Mr Mystery in weeks, not since we had some dessert out in the back alley. Which is weird, he's usually always there Friday night, maybe he got what he wanted and wasn't interested in anything more. It shouldn't bother me, but it does. Not the point though, last night is my point. So, we're at the club, the one my boss owns, having a few drinks, me a lot less than Scarlett. And we decided to start dancing. A girl comes up behind me, no idea who she is. And all of a sudden, she's dancing all over me. I didn't really think much of it at the time, I mean it's happened before when I've gone out with Scarlett to other clubs, not even gay clubs. Girls dance all up on each other. So, we're dancing face to face for a couple of songs, then out of nowhere she pulls me in and kisses me right on the lips.

Now see, that is where I should have pushed her away and gave that typical drunk girl giggle and blown it off. We've all done the drunk girl giggle at some point. And that was totally my plan, but then I didn't. She tasted like strawberries, probably either her lip gloss or drink, I couldn't help but keep kissing her. When her tongue entered my mouth, I felt a wave of pleasure shooting right through me and down to my quim. I wanted her to keep kissing me. I wrapped my fingers through her hair and kept her head from moving. I was not done with kissing her. When she finally pulled back, I could have easily gone right back in, but then she gave me the drunk girl giggle and headed off to dance with another girl.

The thing is, I enjoyed it. I enjoyed it a lot and I shouldn't have. I'm straight, I know I'm straight so then why did I enjoy it? I can't even blame it on the martinis. I only had two at that point. Scarlett said there is this thing called bi-curious. Straight girls fool around with another girl to see what it's like. It's an experience she says. Maybe she's right. I couldn't help but wonder if her mouth tasted that sweet, what other parts of her body did? When Mr Mystery kissed me after devouring my quim, I could taste myself on his tongue. It wasn't a sour taste like I thought it would be. It was sweet. Would another girl taste the same?

Maybe I should decide to be a little more adventurous and see what it would be like to be with a female.
If you can't experiment in your twenties, then, when could you? I'm not saying I would go all the way with a girl; I'm not even really sure how that works. But I could see what it feels like to go down on a girl. Maybe I won't like it, perhaps I will, but at least I would have tried. And you never know I could enjoy it. You know what? I'm going to make a list of all the things I've never done with someone sexually, and then I'm going to do it, like a bucket list only for sex. What I'll do when the list is done, I don't know, but I'll worry about that then. I might not get it all

32

crossed off, but I want to try. Who knows, maybe I'll end up adding to it.

Oh, and Hattie added a new post on her Facebook page, get this, she's having a bridal shower next week. She was talking about how she's so excited for it and how she can spend the night with all of her closest friends that are like sisters to her. Sisters. Meanwhile, her real sister is sitting right here being ignored and hated by everyone. It really pisses me off, especially because one of the girls going is Ali, my former best friend who spilt the beans on my drunken one-night stand to her fiancé. Ali gets to go to the bridal shower and not me. That bitch told everyone on purpose just to cause drama and now she's like a sister to my actual sister? WTF? This is why I don't trust people. Why I don't need people, don't get me wrong, I like Scarlett, most days, but if she disappeared tomorrow, I wouldn't fall apart. It would just be Monday. Why anyone feels they need someone in their life, I'll never understand.

Like marriage, why the hell would you marry someone? Over half of marriages end in divorce anyway, seems like a waste of time and money just to make things more complicated when you break up. I'll stay with being single and having random hook-ups thanks - All the more reason to have a sex list. No boyfriend. No family. Hell, not even really any friends. There's no better time than now to be a little wild and have some fun.

My Sex List

Lesbian Sex
Swallowing a guy
First Black guy
Married man
Anal

Bondage- light
Group sex?

CHAPTER 7

Jan. 24, 2020

Another Friday night working at the restaurant, but this time Mr Mystery is back. He hadn't been here in almost a month, and I was starting to think he was never going to come back. I'm glad I decided to wear a tight black dress that was just as short as my red dress from New Year's Eve. I've been wearing tighter and shorter outfits recently. Scarlett and I were planning a shopping trip next week to get some extra goodies for me. She has convinced me that I need to invest in some lingerie if I was dead serious about my sex list, which I am. Mr Mystery was led to my section, and after grabbing a menu, I headed over.

"Long time no see," I said with a flirty smile as I handed him the menu.

"Hello, Sweetness. I was busy at work, couldn't getaway."

His voice was just as sexy as I remember it being. I couldn't help but wonder what he would sound like with me on my knees.

"What do you do for work?" I asked, instead of what I wanted to say to him.

"What colour are they tonight?" He asked instead, giving a slight nod to my crotch.

"You'll see," I said with a sexy smile of my own.

The heat flooded his eyes, and I knew he wanted me just as badly as I wanted him. The problem was, I didn't think I could wait another four hours before the place was closed.

"I'm sure you're hungry, but maybe you'd like dessert first. I have a break in two minutes."

"I'd love to have my dessert. Where?"

"Our back. Three minutes. Make sure you look up."

With that, I walked away, making sure to sway my hips for him. I wasn't sure, but I could have sworn I heard him moan behind me. I knew I shouldn't be doing this, but I did have a fifteen-minute break coming up, and if we were smart, we wouldn't get caught. The first thing I did was go into the ladies' room and remove my black thong. I knew he would want it. It should bother me that he was once again getting a pair of my underwear and I would be going pantyless for the rest of the night, but it only turned me on more. With my thing tucked away into my dress, I headed outback. The back of the building had an old fire escape all the way up to the roof. We could go part way up and be protected from any wandering eyes.
I had just made my way up about halfway when Mr Mystery was walking down the alley. I leaned against the railing and watched as he looked up. I gave him a flirty smile, and he quickly made his way to the stairs and up to me.

I knew what he wanted, but tonight was also going to be about what I wanted. And what I wanted was his dick in my mouth. As he reached me, I didn't even give him a second before I was gently pushing him back against the wall, putting my mouth close to his, I spoke.

"I believe it's my turn for a taste."

"Be my guest Sweetness." He said with a purr in his voice.

I undid his belt and pants. I could feel him hard already and it was only making me wetter. After freeing his hard-on, I got down on my knees and gave him a good long lick, causing him to moan.

"Pull your dress up and spread your legs nice and wide. Show me my dessert."

I did as he ordered and I found myself getting wetter and wetter by the second. I couldn't wait any more. I needed to taste him. I had never given head before without a condom and I found myself excited to be able to feel his flesh in my mouth.
I wrapped my lips around his tip and gave a little suck, getting his precum in my mouth. It wasn't as sweet like me, but it wasn't sour like I thought either. He tasted good and I wanted more. I took him all the way in my mouth, down to his base. The moan that escaped his mouth was intoxicating.

"Touch yourself. I want to watch as you suck my dick and finger fuck yourself. But don't cum. I want to taste your juices on my tongue again." He ordered with a husky voice.

I moaned at the order and did as was told. I had masturbated before, but always alone. Knowing he was watching and getting turned on even more, only encouraged me. I timed it right so that I would have my finger slide into my quim as I took him deep in my mouth, moaning and sending vibrations of pleasure into him.

"Oh fuck. So sexy." He moaned.

He wrapped his hand in my hair and started to thrust his hips forward. I knew he was getting closer. I could feel him getting harder in my mouth. The feel of his hot flesh against my tongue was driving me crazy. I wanted more of him. I didn't want this to end. And now more than ever I wanted to know what it felt like to have his hot cum in my mouth. I wanted to taste all of him. And I wanted it now.

I picked up my pace, making sure he was all the way inside of my mouth as I did. My added speed encouraged him to pick up the pace with his thrust.

"Fuck, I'm gonna cum. If you don't want it in your mouth, now's the time to move."

My mouth was the only place I wanted it. I moved my hands over to his hips to ensure he wouldn't pull back.

"Oh fuck, you want a drink? I got a big one coming your way."

He picked up the pace with his hips to the point he was just fucking my mouth. And I loved every second of it. Every time his tip hit the back of my throat; I was wishing it could go deeper. I couldn't stop moaning, and when he finally released his hot cum into my mouth, I thought for sure I was going to cum myself right then and there. I felt him pulsing against my tongue and vaguely I wondered what it would feel like deep inside my quim. He continued to squirt rope and after rope of cum in my mouth and I gladly swallowed it all. When his pulsing stopped, I didn't. I sucked on his tip, making sure I got every last drop of him. He hissed at the sensitivity but made no move to pull away. I finally released him when he had gone soft, but I wasn't on my knees for very long.

He grabbed my arms and pulled me up, pushing my back against the wall and lifted my right leg and placed it on the railing next to us. Then he was down on his knees and his tongue was deep inside of me once again. I quickly covered my mouth to prevent a scream that was building from being released. Between playing with myself and having the taste of him in my mouth, I was already on the edge and it wouldn't take much to push me over. He sensed that I was close and he moved his hand and began to rub my clit. I grabbed the railing in an effort to keep myself upright. My legs were shaking from my need and with a powerful force I was cumming. I bit my lip to keep the scream in, but a very long and deep moan escaped. He continued to lick and fuck me with his tongue as I continued to pulse and even after. The sensitivity was insane. I had never cum more than once before, never believed it was possible, but right in this moment I was seriously starting to wonder.

Sensing that I was too sensitive, he stood up and once again pulled me in for a heated kiss. The taste of him on my tongue mixed with the taste of me on his. This caused me to moan once again. I would never get tired of that taste. He pushed himself against me, and I could feel his growing erection once again. He was ready for a whole other round and I would have happily given it to him if I had the time. After a moment he pulled back and we were both breathing heavy.

"Next time, I will be having you in my bed. All night." He promised.

My body tingled at hearing the words next time. He wanted more and I was hoping he wanted it just as badly as I did.

"Can't wait." I said.

He pulled back and we began to fix ourselves quickly. I pulled out my thong and handed it to him. We made our way down the stairs, him holding my hand to ensure I wouldn't trip. A surprisingly gentleman thing for him to do that I did not expect. Once at the bottom, he pulled me in for one last kiss before he turned to leave, but I couldn't help but ask.

"Hey, how many pairs of women's underwear do you have exactly?"

"Including this one. Two. A very sexy red thong." The flirty smirk had my heart fluttering. I didn't know if he was telling the truth, but right now I was all too happy to believe him.

With a wink, he turned and headed off, leaving me with no choice but to go back to work and try to ignore the wetness between my legs. I headed back inside and did everything I could to pretend like everything was normal. I headed over to my purse and checked my phone real quick.
There were texts from Scarlett that I would answer later, but also another text from that same unknown number.

Do you enjoy being a slut? Dirty girls deserve to be punished. I can't wait to punish you, Issy.

I froze. I had received a text from this number before, but I thought it was just a wrong number type of deal. It wasn't unheard of. But now my name was attached to it. Whoever this was, knew my name. This couldn't be a mistaken identity situation. This was for me. Who sent it, I had no idea. I hadn't changed my number when I moved, but now I was thinking I should. I don't know who this was, but I wasn't going to let it get to me. It was probably just Christopher being an ass and punishing me for whatever is going on between him and Hattie. That's all this was. When I go to the mall with Scarlett, I'll change my number and that will be that. I quickly deleted the message and out my phone away. I had to get back to work.

CHAPTER 8

Jan, 29, 2020

Shopping day with Scarlett. Normally I'm not too fond of shopping. I'm not the type of girl that spends hours in a mall just looking around for "fun". But I'm actually looking forward to it today. I've been saving up money for a rainy day, and today I've decided to use some of it to get a few new outfits and some lingerie. I have no idea what Scarlett is going to have me try on, but I'm going to do this with a positive attitude and just let myself have fun. I never really let go with anyone. There's always this wall between us, one I put up. It's better that way. You can't get hurt by someone if you don't fully let them in. A mistake I made with Ali and I don't plan on making it twice. Still, with how busy it's been for me at work it'll be nice to have a down day and just have a bit of fun with Scarlett.

I have no doubt she is going to have some crazy story for me. She always does. I swear that girl lives off drama. There could be a perfectly normal, attractive, put together, rich woman standing in front of her, and her eyes would wander off to the woman wearing a tin foil hat talking to herself. I'm not even joking, I've seen it happen. Not the tinfoil hat part, but the crazy lady talking to herself, yup she's done it. Then what does she do when it so shockingly blows up in her face? Comes running over here to tell me all about it and how she didn't see it coming, and no amount of lectures stops her from doing it all over again.

Even with all of the craziness that she brings, I know she's a good person. It's why I've tolerated her and everything that comes with her.

I am looking forward to changing my number today. I haven't received another text message, which I'm thankful for, but I'll feel better once I have a new number and only Scarlett, my work and my parents will have. I don't even really want to give it to my parents, but if something happened, they need to be able to get a hold of me to tell me. I've also decided that if I am going to be hooking up with random strangers, I need to have a fake name when asked. I'm not too sure it's a good idea to give out my real one to strangers. It sounds silly, considering I would give it to someone on the street or anyone who walks into my work knows my name. Still, it makes me feel a little bit more protected. Besides, chances are I won't be seeing them again anyway.

And there's Scarlett banging at my door.

My Sex List

Lesbian Sex
~~Swallowing a guy~~
First Black guy
Married man
Anal
Bondage- light
Group sex?
"I'm coming!"

She was going to piss off my neighbour again and I was not in the mood to hear another lecture about people my age and ruining the peace around us. I quickly opened the door and Scarlett barged right in, heading over to my kitchen to see what snack she could steal.

"Hello to you too," I said, slightly sarcastic.

"Hey hot stuff. Is that what you're wearing?"

I looked down and saw my jeans, t-shirt and sneakers. I didn't see anything wrong with it but considering Scarlett was dressed as if she was going out to a club, I could see how she would feel I was underdressed. Still, this was just a trip to the mall. I saw no need to look fancy.

"Yes, this is what I'm wearing. You'll survive with my extreme casualness." I said with an eye roll.

"Fine. You ready?"

"Yes."

I grabbed my coat and purse and we were off. Seeing as Scarlett didn't drive, we took my car and headed for the mall.

"How are you and your new girl? Beth, was it?" I asked.

"Oh, we broke up. She was a little too tough for my liking."

She didn't show it, but I could pick up a hint of pain in her voice. Something happened between them, but she wasn't ready to talk yet so I let it go.

"Anyone new?"

"Not yet. But we're going to the club tomorrow so I might find my perfect match. So, you and Mr Mystery, did you get his name yet?"

"Nope. I could ask, but at this point, it seems wrong."

"Wrong how?" Scarlett asked, confused.

"We've already done things together. The time to ask for a name would have been before we hooked up. I'm hoping one day he's just going to let it slip or use a credit card and save me the embarrassment of asking."

"And he hasn't been back?"

"Nope. He only comes in on Fridays, and even recently it hasn't been every Friday.
He said work was busy, but when I asked what he does, he changed the subject."

"Ooh, maybe he works as a spy or something. Like if he told you his real name, he would have to kill you. How crazy would that be?" Scarlett said as she clapped her hands in excitement.

"Only you would find that exciting. And he's not a spy. He's just a private person."

"So private that he doesn't even lie to you and make up a name or a job? Honey, that is being more than private."

"Shut up. And it doesn't matter. I don't need to know his name or what he does. I'm not looking for anything like that."

We pulled into the mall, and after finding a spot to park, we headed in. We hit the phone store first so I could change my number and with that out of the way, the fun could begin. We headed for one of Scarlett's favourite clothing stores to get me some new party clothes.

"Can I ask you something?" I started.

"Only always."

"What do you do when you have sex with a woman? I know up to third base, but what do you do afterwards? Or is that it?"

I know I could have easily looked this up online, but somethings in life you really shouldn't Google. Scarlett was always open to anything sexual, so I knew asking her wouldn't bother her.

"Oh, that's far from it. What happens next depends on who you are with. But there's always toys. Some girls will have a strap on so they can screw you. Some even have a strap on for you and there's a vibrator attached that goes into the other girl so the more she pounds into you the faster the vibrator goes. It makes it so you both can cum together without someone feeling left out."

"Huh, interesting."

"Why do you ask? Are you thinking about having some fun tomorrow night?"

"Maybe."

I wasn't planning anything, but if it came up, I wasn't going to be saying no. Scarlett gave a little squeal and had everyone in the store looking over at us.

"Oh my god, this is perfect. I can set you up with this girl that I know.
She has one of those strap-ons and loves to use it. She also loves newbies. She'll take good care of you, and most importantly, she won't hound you next time. She's totally cool if you want just a one and done type of thing."

"Maybe. I'll see. I'm not really planning anything, but I'm not avoiding it either. I'm just curious, that's all."

"Fair enough. Now we totally need to find you the perfect outfit for tomorrow night."

"And some new panties. Mr Mystery keeps taking mine after each time."

Scarlett snapped around to face me, completely forgetting about the way too short dress in her hands.

"Are you serious? What does he do with them?"

"Yup and no idea."

"What does he have, like a drawer full?"

"I asked him how many he had, he said only two, which are mine. Not too sure I believe that. I mean you don't just randomly start collecting women's underwear one night." That's what I couldn't figure out. What was he doing with them?

"Maybe he's selling them. You wouldn't believe the market for used women's underwear. He could be making money off you and you wouldn't even know it."

"I don't think he's selling them. And what do they do with the underwear after they get it?" Buying used underwear was insane to me. Like really, what would you need it for?

"They smell it. Some guys really like the smell of a woman's quim. So, a girl will wear it and get her juices all over it and then seal it in a bag and sell it for like a hundred pounds apiece. And considering one pair might cost you like four pounds in a store you are seeing insane profits. Talk about a recession-proof business."

"Why do I have a feeling you've done this before."

"Because I have," Scarlett said with a laugh.

"Why?" I don't know why I was shocked. Really at this point anything Scarlett does shouldn't shock me, but this does.

"It's good money. Like I said recession-proof. Don't worry; we'll pick up some extra pairs for when Mr Mystery comes by to take them."

I rolled my eyes and moved on to look at some of the skirts. I tended to like wearing jeans and pants, but I wasn't about to fight to get out of them if I needed quick access. Dresses and skirts were what I needed today. And tomorrow I might just get to try one out.

CHAPTER 9

Jan. 30, 2020

It's four in the morning, and I should be asleep, but my mind won't shut off. I can't stop thinking about what happened tonight, or yesterday I guess, at the club. I ended up wearing this dark red sheer dress that had a couple of dark spots for my nipples and then was normal fabric at the bottom to cover everything below my hips. It was also backless so I didn't wear a bra. I could feel the eyes on me when we walked in, and I knew there were going to be a lot of girls interested in being with me. I could feel the excitement going all through me. I had no idea what was going to happen, but I wanted something to happen. Scarlett and I started to dance and right away, different girls were joining us. Some were prettier than others. But then partway through the night Scarlett's "friend" that she was telling me about showed up and started to dance with me.

Beck, she had long blonde hair, with blue eyes and a beautiful face. She was model pretty. And very much interested in me. After only one dance we were already making out on the dance floor, and our hands were wandering to places that should not be explored in public. We quickly made our way to her car and headed back to her place. Once there, that is when things really heated up...

Her mouth was like fire, and I wanted it to burn me up from the inside. I had only kissed a woman once, but I was finding it to be a very enjoyable sensation. A man's mouth was rough, and often their five o-clock shadow was scratchy. With a woman though, it was all soft and smooth. A stiff contrast to what I was used to, but this was just as pleasurable as any kiss from a man.

She pushed me back, guiding me with her body to her bedroom. Once there, she wasted no time in stripping me of my dress but leaving my shoes on. I removed her black dress, doing the same for her shoes. After a moment she broke the kiss and pulled back to look at me.

"Beautiful. Scar said you hadn't done this before."

"No, I'm just curious," I answered honestly.

She went over to her bed and laid down, spreading her legs a bit and bending them up. "Well then, explore away."

For some reason seeing her like this only turned me on even more. I climbed onto the bed and ran my hand down her body. Going over her breast and not stopping until I reached her fully waxed quim. I didn't touch it though. I wanted to explore other areas first. Leaning forward, I began to kiss all along her neck and made my way down to her right breast.

I flicked my tongue along her nipple before taking it into my mouth and sucking it. I could feel it harden in my mouth and I very gently gave it a little nip. I could tell from the moan that I received that Beck liked it. I showed her left breast the same attention before kissing my way down her stomach.

I kissed my way down to the top of her quim before stopping and looking back up at her.

"Go ahead, taste it. It's nice and juicy for you." Beck spread her legs even more, giving me more access to it.

I wasn't about to back out now, not when I was this close to finding out what it felt like to be with a woman. I moved down and ran my tongue from the bottom of her folds up to her clit. Beck gave a deep moan at the contact. I had a feeling she was getting more turned on by me being a newbie than anything. But in this moment, I didn't care, because her sweet taste was flooding my mouth and all I could think about was wanting more. I ran my tongue along her inside folds once again, but this time instead of going up to her clit, I pushed it a little bit inside of her hole.

"Oh, that's it. Eat my pussy baby girl."

And that's exactly what I did.
I moved my hands so they were on her thighs and I pushed them up so she was spread even wider for me. With her thighs where I wanted them, I then used my hand and spread her folds open fully so I could see her hole. I pushed my tongue in as far as it could go and wiggled it around. I knew I had her when she couldn't stop moaning. I moved my free hand over to her clit and began to rub circles around it. I could feel her insides getting tired around my tongue and I knew she was close to cumming.

All of a sudden, she was pushing me away and I felt ripped off. I wanted to taste her cum. I wanted to see what I would feel like.

"Lay down," Beck ordered as she was already pushing me down on my back.

She climbed on top of me and bent down so she had her feet on the mattress and was squatting right over my mouth. She lowered herself down, so her quim was fully open and sitting on my mouth.

"Eat me baby girl." She ordered, and I didn't need to be told twice.

With the new position I could get my whole tongue inside of her. I could feel her rubbing her clit, and I knew it wouldn't be long before she was exploding onto my tongue.

"Oh fuck, you're a natural pussy eater." Beck moaned.

Her breathing was coming in pants now, and I could feel her tightening inside. Not even a moment later she was cumming with a small scream. I could feel the pulses ripping through her as her cum dripped down onto my tongue and in my mouth. I was doing everything I could to lick up her sweet honey taste. Beck continued to rub her clit, only faster.

"Oh, don't stop. Keep fucking me that that tongue. I got something special for you." Beck ordered.

I had no idea what that was, but I didn't need to be told twice. I could have done this all night and been happy. Her taste was amazing, and I wanted more. I shoved my tongue back inside of her and continued to eat her out. Her body was trembling and she was giving off small screams at the pleasure that was coursing through her.

53

"Oh, I'm close, don't stop. Close your mouth around my pussy; I want you to get every drop. I'm gonna squirt."

I had no idea what she meant by that, but I happily did as I was told. Still licking her insides, I closed my mouth so that I was practically sucking on her quim. Then all of a sudden, she gave a scream of pure pleasure and her cum was squirting into my mouth. I couldn't believe the taste of it.

It was like liquid honey was being poured into my mouth, and it kept coming. The more I licked, the more her juices would shoot out and into my mouth. I wanted more. When the last shot came, she went to get up, but I wasn't having it. I placed my hands on her thighs and kept her down as I continued to lick her up.

"You want more baby girl? I can give you one more. You want one even bigger, put your fingers inside and hit that sweet spot. I'll give you twice as much."

I instantly moved my right hand to insert two of my fingers deep inside of her. She gave out another scream and started to rock back and forth to help me find the right spot. I knew I hit her g-spot when she screamed out. I pounded my fingers into her as I continued to lick her while she was rubbing her clit as fast as she could.

"Oh, that's it. Don't stop. It's building. I'm gonna let it keep building and hold it all in so it's nice and big for you."

I couldn't help the moan, I thought for sure I would cum from the pleasure I was receiving from this alone. And I hadn't even been touched. I have no idea how long we spent doing this, but I felt her getting close, and I knew when to remove my fingers and went back with my tongue. With a loud scream, she was squirting once again into my mouth.

A river flooded my mouth and I swallowed everything that I could. I continued to lick at her until I had every last drop of her sweet juices.

Beck got up off from me and knelt down beside me. My mouth was all wet, and I knew there were some of her juices on my chin. Beck got up as she spoke.

"Spread your legs."

I did as I was told, and Beck went over to grab a strap on. I had no idea if it had a vibrator for her or not, but I had a feeling she would be too sensitive for one. She quickly put it on and then went between my legs. She placed her hands on my inner thighs and pushed them open even more and up so I was bent over myself. Then without any warning, she slammed her nine-inch strap-on inside of me in one go. I couldn't hold back the moan that escaped as I was spread open. Her angle was perfectly catching my g-spot, taking any pain away within a second.

"Rub your clit and don't stop until I tell you to." She ordered as she pounded into me fast and deep.

My body was already sensitive, so I knew that it wouldn't be long before I was cumming. With the added pleasure of me touching my clit I was cumming all too soon. Wave after wave of pleasure shot through me, but even when it passed, Beck didn't stop.

"Keep rubbing your clit. I didn't say stop. I'm going to make you squirt."

"I can't; I've never." I could barely talk right now; I was too overwhelmed by the pleasure going through me.

"Yes, you can. Every girl can. You'll see."

Beck flicked a button on the strap-on, then it began to vibrate at a breakneck pace. I couldn't stop the scream; I found that I didn't want to. The pleasure was overwhelming. It felt like I was going to be swallowed whole by it. I could feel something building inside of me. It also felt like I had to pee, but I knew that wasn't possible. It kept building and building and before I knew it, I was exploding with a scream. My juices shot up every time Beck pulled out. It was hitting my stomach and running out of me. It felt amazing, out of this world. And just when I thought I couldn't cum anymore, Beck proved me wrong.

I had no idea a girl could do that. I mean it sounds crazy, and yet I lived it. I did it. And it felt so unbelievable. And I can't get over the taste of her. Maybe it's my sweet tooth that is talking, but she tasted better than anything I had ever had before. Being completely honest though, I would have been perfectly satisfied if she had returned the favour and that would have been it. The whole strap-on thing, yes it felt good, but I definitely prefer the real deal to the fake.
I think I would be in heaven if I could eat a girl out and get pounded in from behind. I could literally die happy at that point. That's why I'm erasing the question mark from group sex. That needs to be a thing in my life that I experience. I can still taste her on my tongue. I'm not even brushing my teeth tonight. No way am I going to lose this taste, at least not for a few more hours. I'm still straight, but maybe I have an oral fetish? Either way, I'm going to bed with a smile on my face.

My Sex List

~~Lesbian Sex~~
~~Swallowing a guy~~
First Black guy
Married man
Anal
Bondage- light
Group sex

CHAPTER 10

Feb. 17, 2020

You know what really sucks? When work has been so busy, I haven't been able to go out and do anything. All I've done practically this whole month is work. Between working at the restaurant and filling in for shifts at the club, I've been working almost six days a week. And too tired on the seventh day to do anything. With it being winter, everyone is taking a vacation to go off to some tropical destination, except me. I have no interest in sandy beaches thanks. Even Scarlett has been pretty scarce recently. She's apparently back with that girl she felt was too rough at times. Not really sure what the story is there, but my gut is telling me it's nothing good. It's her life though and I have no right to live it. So here I am on a Monday night and I've decided to do something crazy. I'm going out to a club. I doubt it'll be busy, but at least I'll be able to get out and have some fun, hopefully. I seriously need to get laid. I haven't had proper sex with a man in months, like over eight of them. And considering Mr Mystery is a no show once again I haven't been able to do anything with him. So tonight, it's all about finding me a man to pound my brains out. I've even picked out the perfect outfit, a short black skirt that barely covered my ass, and won't cover much when I sit down, with a crop black lace top with just enough lace to cover my nipples. And I'm pairing it with my black stiletto heels.

It was slutty and I loved it. I was really starting to love how I felt and looked in my new clothes. I felt empowered and beautiful. Tonight, was all about sex.

I arrived at the club and headed straight in. Not surprisingly, no one was waiting in line. Though there was a good amount of people inside, It wasn't full, but it wasn't dead either. Apparently, I wasn't the only one that had been working most weekends. I headed down to grab a drink and took a seat. There was a very attractive black man sitting at the bar as well, and he was looking directly at me. I gave him a sexy smirk as I leaned my elbows against the bar top, pushing my breasts up more and giving him more of a view. The heated look that took over his eyes told me that he was enjoying it. My martini came, and he made his way over to sit down next to me.

"Hello, beautiful." He said with a rich-toned voice.

"Hey," I said back with a smile.

I didn't care for small talk tonight. Tonight, was all about one thing and one thing only. Small talk had nothing to do with it.

"You waiting for someone?" He asked.

"Nope. You here with your wife?" I asked, noticing the wedding ring on his finger.

"No, I'm in on business. That a problem?"

"You got a car here?" I asked, instead.

"SUV, out back."

I drank my drink as I got up. "Lead the way."

He gave me a big smile as he took my hand, and we headed out of the club to the back parking lot. He led me over to his black SUV and opened the back door. I got in, and he closed it behind him. I wasn't about to wait for him to make the first move. I grabbed the front of his shirt and pulled him down to me. His lips instantly found mine and the kiss quickly turned heated. I removed his shirt and started to work on his pants. He grabbed the straps of my top and pushed them down my arms, freeing my breasts. His hands instantly went to them both, squeezing and pinching my already hard nipples. A moan escaped, he pushed his tongue into my mouth, thrusting it deep inside. His kiss was all about power, he wanted it, and he loved having it. Not one to care about who is in control, I surrendered to him. This only fuelled him. He pulled my skirt up and ran his hand between my legs. He pulled back from the kiss when he felt that I had nothing on underneath.

"Well, aren't you a naughty girl." He said as he inserted one of his thick fingers inside of my already wet pussy.
I moaned before I could answer. "I'm a girl who knows what she wants."

"And what do you want?"

"I want you to fuck me."

"Ya? With what? My fingers?"

He inserted a second one and began to push them in and out of me at a fast pace. Making sure he hit my sweet spot each time. I spread my legs even more and pushed my hips down on his fingers to get them to go even deeper.

"That feel good?" He asked, already knowing the answer.

"Yes." I breathed, as I rode his fingers.

"Is this what you are after tonight? You want to fuck yourself on my fingers?"

"No." I breathed, as he pushed them even faster into me.

"Tell me what you want to fuck." He demanded.

"Your dick."

I could feel my release building, and as much as I wanted to cum, I didn't want it to be on his fingers. I was after the real deal tonight, that was the only thing I would settle for. I knew he wanted it to; he just wanted to be in control of it all. It was turning him on. His dick was slick from the precum, his tip swollen. He wanted inside of me just as badly as I did. He removed his fingers and held them up to my mouth as he spoke.

"Lick em clean."

I took his two fingers into my mouth and moaned at the taste of myself on them. I looked right at him as I sucked on them and got every bit of juice off from them. I could have sworn his eyes went black from his need. His free hand came up to my neck and held me just under my jaw as he pulled his fingers from my mouth and crushed his down on top of mine. The kiss was even rougher than before, his hold on my neck firm as he ravished my mouth, shoving his tongue inside as deep as he could get it. And I loved it. Being at his mercy was turning me on even more. Not being in control was freeing. Being dominated in this way was freeing.

He pulled back but kept his grip the same.

"Turn around and spread your legs." He ordered, and I gladly obliged.

After I turned around so my back was to him, I spread my legs as far apart as I could, while still up on my knees. With the height of the car, I was more in a raised sitting position on my knees. He got behind me, and I could feel his tip against my hole.

"You want my dick, then fuck it. Show me how much of a naughty girl you are."

I didn't need to be told twice. I lowered myself onto his cock, and I didn't stop until he was fully inside of me. I knew black guys were big, but damn he was huge. Easily a foot long and thick as hell. I could feel the burn as I was stretched to accommodate his girth, but I didn't wait. Once I bottomed out, I pulled back up and slammed back down on him, causing us both to moan. He had his left hand wrapped around the front of my neck, and he threaded his right hand into my hair, pulling it tight and causing my head to go back. I couldn't stop moaning. I had been so rarely this turned on; I loved the control he had over me. I continued fucking myself on his dick, and every time I moved forward the added pleasure of the pull on my hair only made me wetter. I should have been more worried about him not wearing a condom, but the feel of his hot flesh inside of me was driving me crazy. I wanted to feel his hot cum scorching my insides. Just the thought of it made me go faster and all too soon my walls were clenching down; my loud moan filled the car as I came.

He grunted behind me and held me down so I couldn't move. I could tell he was on the edge, but he didn't want to go over yet.

After I stopped pulsing, he let me move once again. The angle we were in was forcing his cock to hit my g-spot, I could feel that liquid building once again. I moved my hand down to my clit and began to rub it. I wanted to squirt. I wanted to see what it would feel like against a real dick. But before I could get there, he let go of my hair and pulled out. Replacing his dick with two fingers. I moaned at the loss of his thickness; he just gave a dark chuckle.

"I'm not done with you yet. It's too early for me to cum."

He moved his left hand from my neck and slapped my ass hard. "Come on, fuck my fingers."

I moaned as he slapped my ass again. Loving the slight sting it brought. I began to ride his fingers as I continued to run my clit, but I was holding myself off. I wanted his dick to feel this, not his fingers. After a few moments, he was back inside of me, his hand at the back of my neck, pulling me even closer to him.

"Oh fuck," I screamed as I could feel myself squirting.

He grunted behind me, clearly shocked at what he was feeling.

"Fuck, you can squirt. Oh, fuck ya you naughty girl, cover my dick with your juices."

He pounded even harder into me and I could feel him losing control. My squirting was clearly pushing him over the edge. His grip on my neck tightened and I briefly wondered if there would be a bruise there in the morning, but I blew it off. It felt way too good to care.

"Don't stop, I'm gonna squirt again, don't stop," I begged.

He was grunting nonstop behind me, I knew he was trying to hold off ejaculating. After a few more passes over my g-spot I was squirting once again and he was cumming hard and deep inside of me. I screamed at the pleasure of feeling the heat of his cum covering my insides. It was one of the best feelings I had ever felt in my life. To feel the heat of every rope that came out of him was unbelievable. And my own squirting out of me. Black spots danced in front of my eyes, I thought for a second I would pass out just from the pleasure alone, but then they cleared as his grip loosened. When he stopped pulsing, he turned me and laid me down on my back. He spread my legs and inserted two fingers once again inside of me. I moaned at the contact of my far too sensitive quim.

He moved them around for a minute before pulling them out, covered in both of our cum, and using his left hand he grabbed my chin to open my mouth, I happily did so, and he shoved his fingers into my mouth.

"Oh, that's it, lick em clean, you naughty girl. Taste us." He said as he felt my tongue going over his fingers.

I wasn't sure about the taste. Mr Mystery and I tasted better, but it wasn't disgusting either. After doing it twice more, he seemed happy and moved back.

"It's a shame I'm only in town tonight. I would have loved a repeat." He said as he put himself away.

I spoke as I fixed myself up. "Maybe next time."

"I'm Mark, what's your name?"

"Cindy." I easily lied.

"Hopefully I'll see you around the next time I'm in town Cindy."

"If you're lucky."

And with that I got out of his SUV and headed back to my car. There was no need to go inside the bar again; after all, I got what I came for. Getting into my car, my phone beeped with a text message. I saw that it was just before midnight and figured it was probably Scarlett. Opening it up, I saw that it was an unknown number once again.

You thought I couldn't find you? A new number won't stop me. I'm going to be seeing you very soon Issy and you will pay for being a slut.

My whole body froze. I had no idea who this was, but it should have been impossible for anyone to have my number. I only gave it to four people, and none of them would send me something like this. I had no idea what was going on or how to stop it. I changed my number on purpose, and now it was happening all over again. What the hell was I going to do?

CHAPTER 11

Feb. 21, 2020

It's been four days since my hook up with Mark, and since then I've received another text message from this unknown person. It seems to be about the same thing, calling me a slut and saying I have to be punished. But punished for what? Having fun? And what right does this person have calling me a slut when I'm just exploring different possibilities. It's not like I'm in some committed relationship and am sleeping around for the hell of it. I'm single, and I'm young, I have every right to be a little adventurous in the bedroom. Or "bedrooms" I guess I should say. Whoever this was, was just a hater and he or she could go to hell. It's probably my sister. I wouldn't put it past Hattie. She's blubbering on and on all over her Facebook page about her Mother's Day weekend wedding. Apparently, she thought Mother's day; March 22nd was a great day to get married. Sure, why not ruin everyone's Mothering Sunday by having to show up for her wedding. Well, she can go fuck herself for this stunt. I'm not going to let it scare me or stop me from having a good time. Tonight is Friday and with a little bit of luck, Mr Mystery will be at the restaurant tonight and up for another round of fun. Only this time I want him in bed. And I'd like to point out how I was able to get a married man and a black man off my list in one go. Worked out pretty well if I do say so myself.

My Sex List

~~Lesbian Sex~~
~~Swallowing a guy~~
~~First Black guy~~
~~Married man~~
Anal
Bondage- light
Group sex

I felt my heart flutter when he walked in just after seven tonight. Mr Mystery looked very good in his black straight cut jeans, his black t-shirt and black leather jacket. I had no idea what he did for a living, but it wouldn't surprise me if he was military or security. I didn't believe in the whole spy theory that Scarlett has, but I could see him being some type of protector. I don't know what it is about him, but just looking at him was doing all kinds of things to my body. He was about to be seated in Jessica's area, but after a quick word, he was placed in mine. I couldn't stop the smile that spread across my face. He knew I worked most Friday nights and he was here for me specifically tonight.

I headed to the ladies' room real quick to remove my dark purple thong and placed it into the pocket of my pants. Then I headed out to see Mr Mystery. He gave me a warm smile as I approached his table. I was fairly confident that I would never tire of seeing it.

"Hello Issy." He said in a purr, I wanted nothing more than to hear him moan my name.

"Hello, whiskey?"

"Yes please. And I'll have the special."

"Coming right up," I said with a flirty smile before I turned and headed off to put his order in.

I made sure to tuck my thong between the napkins and grabbed his drink. Going back over to the table, I placed them both down with a warm smile.

"Here's your drink and your food will be by soon." I gave him a wink and turned away.

I went over to the bar and turned to look at him. He noticed the napkin and lifted it up to see the thong. He gave a devilish smile as he took it and placed it into his pocket. He looked directly at me, I could tell he was more than ready for another round. I busied myself with my other tables as his food was cooking. Once it was ready, I brought it over to him.

"I'll pick you up at eleven. Out front."

"Looking forward to it," I said and headed off to do my job.

I wanted to make sure I got everything done so come eleven I would be able to get out of this place and off with Mr Mystery. And maybe I would actually be able to learn his name.

It was finally eleven, the rest of my shift dragged one once Mr Mystery left after finishing his meal. He gave me a good tip though, like always. Seemed a little weird to tip the person you were about to have sex with, but I'm not one to look a gift horse in the mouth, a twenty-pound tip was a twenty-pound tip. I made my way out front and there he was leaning against his truck. It was a black pickup truck, and I could tell he took very good care of it. I don't know why, but seeing him with a truck surprised me. It shouldn't, considering I knew nothing about him. I quickly made my way over, and he opened the door for me.

"Thanks," I said, as I got inside.

He climbed in and then we were off.

"Where we going?" I asked.

"Not far. There's a hotel right around the corner. I already got us a room."

"A hotel room, eh? Trying to keep me as a dirty secret from the wife?" I teased, but part of me was anxious he was married. Which is insane considering I just slept with a married man. But my heart ached with the prospect that he could very well be married or living with another woman.

He gave a chuckle; it was dark, and rich and I wanted to hear it again. "No nothing like that."

I wanted to ask him more, but my experiences in the past with him told me he wouldn't answer. There was no point in pressing for me when he wouldn't give it to me no matter what. Besides, it didn't really matter. I didn't know his name, so why know anything else about him. We quickly arrived at the hotel, and he parked near the entrance. We got out and headed inside. He turned the lights on and I saw there was only one queen size bed, the comforter was already pulled off it and there on the headboard were four restraints. Mr Mystery planned ahead it would seem. It should have made me nervous, but something about him told me that he wouldn't hurt me.

"I'm hoping you're the adventurous type." He said into my ear from behind me.

"I've never done bondage, but I have wanted to," I said, as I turned around to face him, our bodies touching.

"I should warn you; I'm not a fan of condoms. But I'm clean."

"Me too. And good. I want to feel the heat of your cum inside of me. I hope you can keep up though; you did promise me a night of fucking." I said, with my mouth just millimetres away from his.

"Oh, I can go all night, don't you worry about that. By the time I'm done with you, you'll be so full of my cum; it'll be dripping out of you for days."

And with that promise, his mouth was devouring mine. Unlike Mark, his kiss was heated and full of passion, but not control. He wasn't a man that demanded control, maybe because he knew he already had it -Either way I welcomed his tongue inside my mouth and his hands on my body.

The kiss quickly turned heated, he ran his hands down my back and cupped my ass. I wished I hadn't worn pants tonight, but I had no idea if he would show. He made quick work of removing me of my clothing, leaving him fully dressed. He pulled back from the kiss and looked me right in the eyes as he ran his hand down my body to the insides of my folds.

"You're soaking wet Sweetness. Should I lick it up?"

"Oh god." I moaned.

"Say it. Tell me what you want me to do to your sweet quim." He said as he inserted a finger inside of me.

"Lick it."

"You want to feel my tongue inside of you again?"

"Yes." I all but begged because god did his tongue feel amazing buried inside of me.

"I think I could do that."

And with that, he picked me up from the bottom of my ass and brought me over to the bed. He placed me down and then grabbed my right wrist and attached it to one of the restraints on the post. He did the same to the left. He suddenly grabbed my right ankle and attached it to the other restraint on the post and did the same to my left. When he was done, he sat back and took me in. Both of my hands were restrained, but with how he attached the other restraints to my ankles, he left me completely exposed and at his mercy, my legs were bent and spread as wide apart as my body could handle - Leaving nothing to the imagination. I should have felt exposed, but instead, I was only turned on. I could feel myself getting wetter just thinking about what he was going to do to me.

He made a show of slowly getting up from the bed to remove his own clothing. Once he had his removed, he strode back over to me, his hard-on clear for me to see.

He gave me a smirk as he bent down and didn't even waste a second before his tongue was diving deep inside of me. I moaned at the sensation, pulling on the restraints just slightly.

"You taste so good, Sweetness. I could do this all night."

I would have let him, genuinely would have let him. He was so unbelievably talented with that tongue of his; he should seriously teach a class to other guys on how to do this. He inserted a finger and very quickly found my g-spot. But instead of fucking me with it, he rubbed circles over it, as he continued to lick and suck on my clit. I had very quickly turned into a moaning mess there on the bed. All too soon I was cumming against his tongue, and he happily lapped it all up. I was hoping he would keep going so I could squirt, my new favourite thing, but instead he stopped and moved up, so his erect cock was right in front of my mouth.

"I'm going to fuck you, but first I'm going to fuck this sweet mouth of yours."

"It's a good thing I'm thirsty then," I said playfully.

"I got a big drink for you."

I opened my mouth, and he slid right into it, not stopping until he hit the back of my throat.
I gave a deep moan, and he didn't hold back. He fucked my mouth fast and deep, I loved every second of it. Hearing him moan and groan as he got pleasure from my mouth. It was only turning me on more. I could feel him getting closer, when he finally gave a deep moan, saying my name, he came hard and

deep, his cum hitting the back of my throat. I swallowed everything he had to offer me and even when he started to go soft, I continued to suck. He gently rocked his hips back and forth, letting himself catch his breath. Once I had him hard again, he pulled back. He moved down between my legs and rubbed my clit with the tip of his erection.

"You ready for me, Sweetness?"

"Please." I moaned. I was more than ready. Had been since the moment I met him. This was long overdue.

"Not until you tell me what you want." He was playing, we both knew it, but I had a feeling he wasn't going to give in, not until I did.

"I want you."

"To do what?"

"I want you inside of me."

"Yeah, like my finger?"

"No, your dick inside of me."

"Yeah? Inside where? That mouth of yours again?"

He moved his tip down to my folds and continued until he hit my ass. He rubbed his tip over my hole as he spoke. "Or maybe you want my dick to fill your tight ass first."

"You know where I want it."

"You gotta say it. Come on, Sweetness, say it and I'll give it to you."

"I want your dick inside my pussy."

"As you wish."

That was the only warning I had before he was shoving everything; he had inside of me. I screamed out in the pleasure of feeling him spreading me open and filling me up.

"So tight and wet." He moaned.

I moaned as he pulled all the way out only to shove himself right back in.

"You want it slow or hard and deep, Sweetness?"

"Hard and deep. I need it so bad." the very last thing I needed was slow right now.

He didn't need to be told twice as he started at a brutal pace. He was going as fast as hc could, and making it as deep as he could, and yet it wasn't deep enough. I wanted to feel more of him, more of his heat. I wanted to feel his cum all the way inside of me.

"Deeper." I moaned.

He pulled out, and I gave a whine at the loss. He reached over and pulled on the restraints for my ankles. He made the leash shorter, pulling my hips up off the mattress, folding me in half essentially. He repositioned himself on top of me and then pounded straight down inside of me. Going deeper than anything I had ever felt before.

"Oh yes, fuck, don't stop." I moaned.

"Fuck, I'm gonna fill you up and love knowing that you'll be feeling me inside of you for days." He grunted.

"Yes, yes, fill me up. I want to feel it." I begged.

He reached under the pillow and pulled out a little clamp. I had no idea what it was, but then he was attaching it to my clit and turning it on.
I felt the vibrations flooding my already sensitive body, and I couldn't stop the small scream that came out of me.

"Only a small scream, that won't do. Let's turn it up all the way shall we Sweetness?" He turned the small dial all the way to ten, causing me to let out a loud scream.

"That's better."

He was back to pounding into me, hitting my g-spot dead on each and every time. I could feel that all too familiar building happening inside and I knew I was going to be squirting at any moment.

"Don't stop. So close, fuck don't stop." I begged as my body shook.

I was trying to hold off, knowing it would feel even better when I do, but it came over all of a sudden, I was squirting right up into the air. He gave a deep groan at the sensation, I could see the heat flooding his eyes.

Thanks to the position I was in, some of my liquid juices ended up getting me in the face. Which only turned me on even more.

"Oh fuck, you're getting covered in your sweet juices. Lick your lips, taste yourself." He growled.
I did as I was told and couldn't help the moan that escaped. My whole body felt amazing in this moment. I never wanted it to end.

"I'm gonna make you squirt again. I'm going to have you soaked in your own juices." He growled.

"Oh, fuck, yes. I want to shower in it. Oh, fuck so good."

I sounded like a whore, I did pick up on that, but fuck it. My whole body was tingling. Even my teeth felt like they were shivering. This man was able to do things to me, make me feel things that I didn't even know existed.

"You're getting closer. I can't feel it building inside of you. Squirt for me, Sweetness."

He pounded deep inside of me, hitting my g-spot relentlessly and all too soon I was squirting again. I was quickly becoming soaked in it, and I loved it. His pace was even faster now, he was reaching the end of his limit, and after another thrust, he buried himself deep inside of me and cam hard. His hot cum made me cry out in ecstasy as I came with him. When we both stopped pulsing and were able to catch our breaths, he slowly started up once again.

"I'm nowhere near done with you."

And that was a promise he more than fulfilled.

CHAPTER 12

Mar. 3, 2020

I'm an idiot! An absolute idiot! An idiot who is late and I don't mean time-wise, I mean my period. It's late. I've never been late before and yet this time around it's late. This is what I get for having random sex without a condom. I should have been on the pill, I'm so stupid. Why didn't I think about that complication before I started having unprotected sex? Now here I am, after peeing on a stick having to wait to see if a stupid plus sign shows up or not. I can't believe I did this to myself. What the hell am I going to do if I'm pregnant? Even worse, who would be the father? Mr Mystery or Mark, the married businessman? I don't even know which one would be worse. And my family?

Huh, I can hear the lectures now. This is what you get for being promiscuous. This is what happens when you don't think ahead. Now you have ruined your good name and your life. They will be bringing up this kid from now until the day I die. I'll never hear the end of it. How the hell am I even supposed to work? Yeah, I could until the baby is born, but then what? What do I do when I go back to work? I live in a one-bedroom apartment. I don't even know if I could afford a two-bedroom. Plus, everything else a baby needs. I don't even really like kids all that much. Don't get me wrong I don't hate them, but I know nothing about babies. I'm the youngest, and I never even babysat in my life.

I know better than this. I was letting myself get caught up in the feelings and in the sex that I allowed myself to forget about what could happen. An oops that will drastically change my life. It could be nothing though. I mean people are late all the time by a week it happens. When I first got my period, it moved around all the time in the month. This could just be because I've been stressing out from these stupid text messages. They are coming in more and more frequent. Now I get one every other day, and they are only getting worse. The last one I got was yesterday, telling me about how they couldn't wait to see my blood. I have no idea what the hell is going on, but I'm sick of it. I know it has to be Hattie or Christopher trying to pay me back, but enough is enough already.

I left Birmingham to start a new life, not to have that old life follow me here. I needed to put an end to it, and I needed to figure out what the hell I'm going to do if I'm pregnant. I wonder if I can keep this from my family. Maybe they won't notice, and when the kid turns eighteen, it can be like this little surprise. Or technically big surprise. Oh, I'm so screwed.

Finally, the timer went off. How ridiculous is it that you have to wait so long before you can find out? I mean it should be simple, pregnant or not pregnant. How complex could it really be? And... oh thank fuck, negative sign. I'm good, I'm in the clear. My period is just late from being stressed and overworked; that's all. I just need a day to relax and I'll be good to go. First things first though, I'm going to the clinic down the street and getting on the pill. No more false alarms. I cannot go through this again. If I'm going to be playing around without a condom, I need to be on the pill and take one worry out of the equation. I can't do this again.

CHAPTER 13

Mar. 14, 2020

It's the weekend, a time where you hang out with your family and friends, but not me, nope. I am currently sitting at my desk writing in my diary like a loser. I did get a lovely visit this morning in the form of a crying Scarlett. Always a fun time at six in the morning. I can't blame her too much though; I did foolishly give her a key. She came jumping into my bed, crying hysterically about her once again ex-girlfriend. They had broken up a few weeks ago. Apparently, the Ex had been rough with her in the past, and now rumours were going around the gay community about it. Some believed her ex that Scarlett had started it all and others believed that Scarlett would never start a physical fight. I had noticed a difference in her in the past few months. She seemed to have lost a little bit of her sparkle that she always had. Now that I know she had been dealing with a bit of domestic violence, I could understand now why she had been different. I am glad that she told me and I'm glad that she is not going to get back with her ex and has been avoiding her. Still, the rumours were hard on her. Having her friends look at her a little different, not too sure which side to believe. It was a crappy position to be in. After talking for a few hours, she headed out to spend some time with her family, which was super unusual for her, leaving me all alone.

In the past, I'd enjoy attending a family dinner over at my parents' house; we were expected to participate in every other week. But now I'm the outcast, so I get no invite, even when my sister is set to be married next Sunday. Not even one text or phone call since I moved here. The only updates I get on them is through Hattie's Facebook page, which she has thankfully still not realised I have access to. I've seen all the pre-wedding photos of them. Her bridal shower, her making the decorations and goody bags for the guests. I knew come next Sunday it would be overflowing with the actual wedding photos. I am not ashamed to admit I'm hoping her dress is ugly and she looks fat in it. But I'm not going to sit around here all weekend and mope. I'm getting ready to go out and have a wild time. There are only two things left on my list, and one of them would be getting crossed off tonight.

My Sex List

~~Lesbian Sex~~
~~Swallowing a guy~~
~~First Black guy~~
~~Married man~~
Anal
~~Bondage- light~~
Group sex

The club was packed, even for early on a weekend.
I thought for sure I would be coming into a half-empty club. I was thrilled to see that it was packed, there were a lot of possibilities for me. I made my way down to grab a drink before I took a look around at the patrons. Everyone seemed to be with someone, either family, friends or a date. I had no idea who I was looking for, but I knew I needed a man. Tonight, I was

wearing a very short spaghetti strap black dress with my red stiletto heels, and once again I decided to forgo the undergarments. They really did get in the way. And I was now down three pairs thanks to Mr Mystery. I decided that standing around here looking all alone and pathetic was not going to work. So, I made my way over to the dance floor and started to dance. My prayers were answered when a pair of strong arms wrapped around my waist.

"You are far too sexy to be out here all alone." A husky voice said into my left ear.

I turned my head just enough to be able to see him. He was tall, close to six feet, had a square jaw and a very thick French accent. He was good looking though, that was all I needed.

"Why don't you keep me company then." I said in a sultry voice.

"I'd be happy to, You got a name?"

"Melissa."
I didn't bother asking him; it wasn't important to me. I went back to dancing, making sure my ass was right against his growing hard-on. I wanted him to know exactly what I was here for. Thankfully after three songs, he got the picture.

"Why don't we take this dance and go someplace else?" He suggested.

"Your place close by?" I asked.

He gave me a big smirk as he spoke. "Let's go."

He grabbed my hand and all but dragged me out of there. I easily followed, and once in his car we were off. After a short ten-minute drive, we were in his house, my back against the front door as he ravished my mouth. We made quick work on removing each other's clothing, me leaving my heels on. His erection sprung to life once it was free from his black slacks. His hands wandered all over my body as he backed me up to his bedroom. Once there, he reached for my wet folds, and I stopped him.

"You can't have that."

I could see the confusion and disappointment all across his face. I couldn't blame him. I did agree to come back to his place. Sex was inevitable. I grabbed his hand and brought it around to my ass, moving it so his finger touched my hole.
"But you can have that."

A light-filled his eyes as he finally understood what I wanted. Leave it to a straight man to always want to have anal sex.

"You sure?" He asked, barely containing his excitement.

"Yes. I'm crossing it off my bucket list. You ever done it?"

"A bunch of times."

"Looks like I picked the right man then."

"Darling, you have no idea. Get on all fours; I need to stretch you out a bit before my dick can fit in you."

I got onto his bed, in the position he wanted me in as he went and grabbed some lube. He came over and bent down behind me, spreading my cheeks open. And then he did something I wasn't expecting. He licked my hole and pleasure shot all the way through me. I couldn't keep the moan in. He continued to lick at my hole and when his tongue slid inside, that is when my arms gave out and I collapsed down onto my elbows, arching my back even more. He continued to eat my ass, I continued to be a moaning mess on the bed.

"So sweet. Hold your cheeks open for me." He ordered.

I did as was told, hearing the pop of the lube lid. He poured some of two of his fingers and then using his index finger, he rubbed some of my hole. I did my best to ignore the cold sensation, hoping that it would get warmed up from being on my skin.

"Last chance." He said.

"Don't stop." I moaned in anticipation.

He slowly inserted his index finger knuckle by knuckle inside of me. I knew that I needed to stay relaxed, or it would be harder for both of us. Once the last knuckle was in, he stopped and gave me a moment to adjust, something I was very thankful for. With a nod from me, he pulled out and slowly pushed back in. It was a weird sensation, one I wasn't too sure I was really getting much pleasure in. My hope was that once I was loosened up enough that his dick would make it feel amazing. After a few minutes of just one finger, he then started to insert the second. This time it did sting, but he once again waited for me to adjust before he began to move them around. Not out, but in a scissoring motion to try and stretch my insides. It was a weird

84

feeling, but after a moment I got used to it. As he moved his fingers in and out of me, his free hand went to my clit and started to rub it, causing me to moan.

I let my mind think about the pleasure I was getting from my clit, and it loosened me up enough for him to get a third finger inside of me. This time the stinging only lasted a few seconds before he was pumping all three fingers in and out of my ass as he slowly rubbed my clit. I wanted more sensation. I wanted him to pick up the pace on my clit and let me cum, but he was making sure I got nowhere near the edge. I started to rock my hips back and forth, hoping for some added friction with my clit, but he pulled his hand away.

"When you cum, my dick is going to be inside your ass, and you will be withering beneath me."

I let out a small whine, knowing I wasn't going to be able to cum anytime soon. He pulled his fingers out and then covered his erection with a generous amount of lube. He then lined himself up with my ass.

"You ready for me?"

"Hell yes."

I had no idea if this was going to be feeling any better, but I was hoping it would. He very slowly pushed the head of his dick inside of me, and the burn was on a whole different level. It reminded me of the first time I had ever had sex when your body was so tight, no amount of stretching was ever going to help. But I took comfort in knowing that like the first time I had sex, it did get better once I got used to it.

My Frenchman thankfully went slow and took his time inching forward. I have no idea how long it took, but eventually, I felt his balls hit my ass. His hands were gripping my hips tightly, I knew he was struggling with himself to stay still. His dick was in a tight, hot space and he wanted nothing more than to pound into me. I got it, and I appreciated him waiting. After a moment when the stinging subsided, I gave a nod, and he pulled back all the way to his tip and then once again pushed back in. He did that a few times at a slow pace, allowing my body to accommodate his size.

He pushed my legs even further apart, forcing me lower onto the bed, my clit just a fraction from touching the comforter.

"You ready to scream?" He asked as he slapped my ass, causing me to moan.

"You think I will?" I teased.

"Oh, you will, they always do."

And with that, he was off. He picked up his pace and began to thrust as deep as he could in me. With the new position, he hit something inside of me that caused me to let out a long moan. I had no idea what that was, but if he kept hitting it, I would happily take it.
Between him hitting that spot over and over again dead on and slapping my ass, I felt like I was going to explode. I needed to cum. I moved my hand down to touch my clit, but before I could, he was slapping it away.

"Who said you could touch? You have to let it build. It's even better when you cum without being touched."

He put my hand back up in front of me and pounded into me even harder. I couldn't help the scream that escaped, and I heard him chuckle darkly behind me. I had proved his point, and he was going to make me prove it over and over again before he was through with me. I didn't care. My whole body was trembling with the need to cum. I could feel it building, but without any contact, it couldn't go over that edge. I knew he was close. I could feel his thrusts becoming more erratic. His breathing was coming in pants now, and I wondered if he would give in and touch me just to bring me over the edge.

"So tight. You like having a dick up your ass?" He moaned.

"Yes, fuck I need to cum."

"So cum, but don't touch."

"I have to," I whined.

"No you don't, Just feel."

He hit that spot inside of me once again, I screamed even louder than before. He focused all of his energy now on hitting that spot dead on. The explosion was building and finally, after another hit, I erupted into one very powerful orgasm. I just in time turned my head into the mattress and let out a loud scream as I felt myself violently cum, pulse after pulse. I never thought it was going to end, and the more he hit that spot inside of me, the more I came. I was still cumming when he finally found his release, shooting his hot cum inside me. I felt his body collapse on top of me as he pulsed deep inside of me. This was better than I had ever expected.

CHAPTER 14

Mar. 22, 2020

Today is the day of the wedding, and here I am once again sitting all alone in my home. I still can't stop thinking about last Saturday night and how amazing it was. I was a little sore the next day, but nothing too crazy. And I will be doing that again another day. Maybe with Mr Mystery. I bet he'd be amazing at it. I should stay in tonight and just wallow in self-pity, but I have the night off, and tomorrow off, so I'm going to enjoy it and go out. I have no idea what I'm going to do or what will happen, but with only one thing left on my list I'm going to try and accomplish it. I might not succeed, but at least I tried. And at least I got out of the house and didn't sit here feeling sorry for myself. Scarlett was still over at her parents' place so it wasn't like I could invite her over or out. I was on my own again tonight, but I was good at being alone. I'm an expert at it really.

I can't decide if I want to look at Hattie's Facebook page or not. I know there is going to be an endless supply of wedding photos coming soon. And I know there will be pre-wedding photos of her getting her hair and makeup done. Despite how they treated me, I still wish I was there. Part of me wants to feel like a family again, and another part of me wants her to catch Christopher screwing the caterer. It's a low blow I know, but still, it would serve her right.

Though, she's so blinded she'll probably take him back and still marry him. That's Hattie for you.

I'm not going to look. I'll save that for next Sunday when I can see all of the wedding pictures while I'm eating my way through a tub of ice cream. That doesn't sound pathetic at all. For now, a nap and then a shower before I head out. Here's hoping my list is completed tonight.

My Sex List

~~Lesbian Sex~~
~~Swallowing a guy~~
~~First Black guy~~
~~Married man~~
~~Anal~~
~~Bondage- light~~
Group sex

I decided to go to a different club tonight, one that maybe would bring out more couples. Tonight, I was wearing a skirt and a crop top, something simple and easy to get in and out of. I was happy to see that the club was busy despite it being Sunday. I would have figured it would be dead, but thankfully not everyone is that invested in Mother's day, and they need something to do. After grabbing a drink, I took in the crowd. I needed to find a couple that seems open to the idea of having another join them.

I'm not really sure if a threesome counts as group sex technically, but to me it does. Maybe later on if I'm feeling more adventurous, I'll add in other people. It's almost impossible though to look at people and tell if they are interested in a threesome though, so I headed off to the dance floor.

It took me three martinis and twenty songs to finally catch the eye of a couple closer to my age. The girl had long brown hair with a streak of blue in it that matched her blue eyes. She was about my size in height and weight. The man held some muscles to him and stood about half a foot taller than her. She was grinding all over him but looking at me. I continued to move my hips to the beat as I looked right at them. Giving them a flirty smile. She gave me a wink and continued to use her man as a pole. He seemed to have caught on, because he was now almost watching me as he ran his hands over her breasts, giving them a squeeze before he moved down to her bare legs and disappear under her short skirt. The girl did a come here motion with her finger, and I easily moved over to them.

I began to dance facing the girl as he both went down to the floor with our legs open, our skirts riding up. She ran her hands up my legs and underneath my skirt. She gave me a sexy smile when she discovered there was nothing else underneath. He both stood back up, she pulled me closer to her and placed her hand on my ass.

"No panties, a bold move. I like it." She said, as she grabbed my right hand and brought it underneath her own skirt. Where I discovered, she didn't have anything else on either.

"Looks like I'm not the only one wet," I said against her ear, causing her to moan.

"You looking to have some fun tonight?" The man asked.

"Only if I can play with you both," I said with a sexy smile.

"Oh, we can make that happen. What's your name?" He asked.

"Skylar."

"I'm Jay, this is my wife, Christy. What kind of fun are you looking for?" Jay asked.

"The kind that lets me eat her out while you pound into me from behind."

I could have tiptoed around that and gone for something sexier. But I was a woman on a mission tonight. I was going to have a better night than Hattie or my family.

"Fuck yeah. We got a place right upstairs. You in?" Christy asked.

"After you," I said.

Christy pushed away from her husband. I followed them around to the back of the club and up to the apartments. Even though we weren't in the club anymore, I could still hear the music blaring from downstairs. Once inside, I was led to the bedroom where Christy wasted no time in removing her clothes, leaving her shoes on.

"You are wearing too much clothes." She said, as she came over to me and removed me of mine.

"We have one rule, no kissing," Jay said.

"Fine with me." if that was the only rule, I'd gladly take it though it seemed like a bit of an odd rule.

Jay removed his clothing and Christy got on her knees and turned to look at me.

"Help me get him hard."

I bent down, and together we ran out tongues along his half-hard shaft. It only took two licks from us before he was fully erect. Christy took him in her mouth while I busied myself by sucking on her nipples and rubbing her clit.
It didn't take long for her to be a moaning mess on the edge. Jay pulled Christy off his dick and ordered us onto the bed. Christy laid with her head by the pillows and spread her legs for me. I went to in between them, but she stopped me.

"Turn around; I want your sweet pussy over here."

I knew what she was after, and I gladly turned around so we could sixty-nine each other. With us in the middle of the bed, there was still enough room for Jay to eventually get behind me. With her legs spread wide, I had full access to her quim, and she pushed my hips down so my legs were spread wide and my pussy was right at her mouth. She wasted no time in going to town on me. Her tongue was everywhere, and all I could do was focus on doing the same to her. She tasted just as sweet as Beck did, and I had no issues shoving my tongue deep inside of her. When i felt the bed shift, I knew Jay had joined us.

"Fuck, you both are so hot eating each other out. I'm gonna blow before I even get in you." Jay moaned.

I looked back and saw that he was jerking off, I had a feeling he needed to rub one out first. I went back to my sweet tasting girl and let him get himself back under control. He slapped my ass a few times before giving a grunt, and I felt his warm cum on my ass.

I moaned as he ran his finger over it and spread my ass cheeks with his one hand and rubbed his cum over my hole. I couldn't help but push my hips back slightly so the tip of his finger went in.

"Oh, you like that, eh?" He asked as he gathered more cum and did it again.

"Fuck yeah." I moaned.

- I knew I would be sore and having anal sex was not what I was looking for tonight, but it did feel good. He slowly inserted his index cum covered finger inside of my ass and began to fuck me with it slowly. Between the finger and Christy eating me out like a champ, I was a goner. I came hard, and Christy licked everything up that I had to offer. I had a little nip on Christy's clit, and she was cumming right behind me with a scream. I liked at her juices like it was the last drink I as ever going to have. Jay's finger was pulled out, and then he was slamming into my pussy. I screamed with pleasure as he went deep inside of me. Christy, recovered from her orgasm, began to lick at my clit, sending shockwaves of pleasure through me.

"This what you want?" Jay asked, slapping my ass once again.

"Yes, so good, don't stop." I moaned.

"Don't stop eating that pussy, not until I tell you to," Jay ordered.

I moved my hands to Christy's hips so I could lift her up slightly. I wanted better access, and with his ass off the mattress, I was able to get full access to her quim. And I was rewarded with a very deep moan from her. I fucked her with my tongue, loving the sweet taste every second of it. I could feel Jay every now and then pulling out and shoving it into Christy's mouth. Feeling his dick going in and out of me was only driving my pleasure up higher. I could feel that all too familiar liquid building inside of me. Christy was a moaning withering mess underneath me, and before I even knew it, she was squirting herself right into my mouth. The sensation caused me to go over the edge, and I felt my own juices shooting out of me. Covering Jay's dick and dripping down into Christy's mouth.

"Shit, you squirt too. Fuck how did I get so lucky to have two girl squirters." Jay said, now pounding even deeper and faster into my ass.

My and Christy continued to eat the other out, lapping up every drop we have to give. After squirting two more times each, Jay quickly pulled out of me.

"Turn around, quick." He ordered.

Both Christy and I did as we were told and Jay jerked himself off for a second before he was cumming on our faces. I had never had what was called a facial before, and I was finding that I liked it. We opened our mouths to catch any that came in. I was glad when I could get a taste of him. He squeezed the last drop he had down directly on my tongue before he slapped my cheek with his softening dick. I swallowed what was in my mouth before turning to Christy. I ran my tongue along her cheek, licking up the cum left there.

"Shit so sexy." Jay moaned.

Christy returned the favour, and we continued until the cum was completely gone. And with that, the last thing on my list was finished. But what was waiting on my phone was anything, but pleasant.

Dirty sluts that take married men to bed deserve to be sliced open. I can't wait to feel your blood between my fingers Issy.

CHAPTER 15

Mar. 31, 2020

I can't believe my car is still in the shop. They said it would only take a day to repair and now it's been three days. Three days of having to take the bus everywhere. At eleven o'clock at night, all I want to do is go home, take a hot shower and go to bed. But instead, I'm stuck sitting on the bus waiting for my stop just so I can walk three blocks home. I'm calling the repair shop tomorrow, and they better have my car fixed. I am not doing this again for another day. It has now been a week since the wedding, and so far, I have received nothing from any family member apart from a few unrelated texts from mom. I know they got married, I saw the sickening photos blasted all over Facebook about them. Gag. But you would think after all of these months now they would have broken and reached out. Like a "Hey, how are you? It's nice to know you are still alive." You know anything like that really. But nope. Now the happily married couple is off on their honeymoon. Will they forget all about how he cheated on her with her own sister. How many margaritas do you need for that?

On to other news. I am still getting creepy and disturbing text messages from someone. And by someone, I mean a member of my family. Still not cool.

I've thought about reporting them, but that seems like it would only cause more problems between my family and me. So, I've resorted to saving them so that one day if I ever need them, I'll have em. It's annoying and disturbing sometimes, but I guess I should be thankful that someone in my family is reaching out to me in a way. A very disturbing and psychotic way, but it's a start, right?

As for my sex life, it's come to a halt for now. I have finished my list, and now I need to come up with a new one. I probably don't need a list, but I like having it. It's important to have goals, right? Mr Mystery was not at work again tonight. I haven't seen him in a month now. I'm almost worried, but it's not my place to be worried. He's a grown-ass man and seems perfectly capable of protecting himself. It's not like we were dating, only having fun. We had some good times, three fantastic times, and now he's moved on to something new and exciting. It happens. So then why do I have this pain in my chest at the thought of him never coming around anymore? It's all so stupid and confusing. And I'm doing what I do best and ignoring it. I have walls around me for a reason, and I was not about to let anyone, especially a man, passed them. I will come up with a new list and continue my journey into discovering who I am and all the things that I like to do. And who knows, maybe he'll be around to help me cross off some of the things on that list.

Finally, it was my stop, and I got off the bus. It wasn't too cold out tonight, and it wasn't raining, something I was eternally grateful for. I made the short walk back to my place and headed inside. I went to unlock my door, only to find it opened. I didn't think much of it. The door was still closed, so Scarlett was most likely in my home drinking and snorting something off my coffee table. I walked inside and saw that it was dark. Scarlett must have been in my bed. I flicked the lights on by the door, and I instantly froze. My living room, dining room and kitchen were completely destroyed. Everything on the shelves was on the floor, dishes shattered with glass everything. Every photo I had up; all three of them were ripped apart. The coffee table was in pieces, the windows all had one-word spray painted all over them, SLUT. My heart was in my chest. I couldn't believe all of this. My home was destroyed, but that's not what caused my panic to rise. No, it was the piece of paper attached to my wall with my butcher's knife holding it in place. One sentence, eight words, and my heart was in my throat. Tears filled my eyes at the reality that I could be wrong about all of this.

I'll be seeing you soon, you dirty slut.

Printed in Great Britain
by Amazon

54586202R00057

The Erotic Diary of Isabelle
The Raunchy Red Book

By: Dianne Rose & Derrick Andre
For Literally Lovesick

Table of Contents